A Few Seasons

Howie Groff

illustrated by Olya Bond

ISBN 978-1-63972-379-9 (Hardcover)
ISBN 978-1-63972-376-8 (Paperback)

Psalm 139:14
I praise you because
you made me in an amazing
and wonderful way.
I know this very well.
– International Children's Bible

Dedication

For my son Gavin. You are my inspiration and so much more.

- Howie Groff

For my small Family. Thank you for your endless support and trust in my new starts!

- Olya Bond

Oh, lucky day–
the wind was just right.
Ky and his sister
love flying their kite.

It is their special time
to imagine new things.
Kate said "Higher!"
as Ky held the string.

"Let's rhyme to life–
a pine tree with spirit."
"We'll name him Gavin."
"Sounds great, let's hear it."

When spring arrived
With planting time
Little Gavin looked up
At the full-grown pines.

Gavin wished:

To grow big and strong—
To be special and belong.

The runt of the litter
Small Gavin was teased
For his short stature
And knotty knees.

But Gavin had courage
With a difficult start
He looked to the future
With hope in his heart.

Not much had change,
As the years went by
The others would heckle
And Gavin would sigh.

Just when he thought
That he'd had enough
Robyn came by
To cheer him up.

"Don't worry Gavin
I've seen the whole thing
It is simply amazing
What A Few Seasons can bring."

Gavin still wished:
    To be big and strong-
    To be special and belong.

Seven years passed
And Christmas had come
They all have looked perfect
That is, but one.

The first tree was chosen
And then the rest
Till our Gavin was left
With his friend and her nest.

Farmer loved Gavin
So, year after year
He would care for his tree
As Christmas drew near.

His needles filled in
And brown turned green
He was the grandest tree
You had ever seen.

Those who saw him
Said "he looks FINE
But our house is too small
For your beautiful pine"

Farmer thought hard
And talked to the mayor
In the center of town
Was a spot that was bare.

"He is perfect—
I completely agree
Our town is in need
Of your wonderful tree."

With a truck and crane
They had to move fast
Christmas Eve Day
Just would not last.

He thought of his past
Easing his fear
Gavin trusted Farmer
Though his future unclear.

His wish was granted:
To be big and strong-
To be special and belong.

Made in the USA
Columbia, SC
12 November 2022

70505444R00018